OLIVER TWISTED

A FESTIVE TALE, FEATURING
RENOWNED THIEF-TAKER &
INVESTIGATOR OF DARK DEEDS &
MAGICAL MAYHEM, JUDAS ISCARIOT

MARTIN DAVEY

This is a work of fiction. Names, characters, places, and incidents either are the product of the author's imagination or are used fictitiously. Any resemblance to actual persons, living or dead, events, or locales is entirely coincidental.

Copyright © 2020 by Martin Davey

All rights reserved. No part of this book may be reproduced or used in any manner without written permission of the copyright owner except for the use of quotations in a book review. For more information, address:
adam@strangemediagroup.com

This paperback edition November 2020

Cover design by Jem Butcher Design
Published by SMG

www.strangemediagroup.com

ISBN: 9798564329972

For Bear and Boo,
who help me to see the world differently
each and every day

CONTENTS

1	Red Snow	1
2	The Winning Paw	5
3	The Spirit of the Three	9
4	Sikes	15
5	Lord Dodger	20
6	The Rookery	26
7	Turn and Turn About	34
8	Littlewing	38
9	Dickens	44
10	Watching the Watchers	50
11	Fright then Flight	53
12	Good Bad Luck	61
13	Royalty and Sausages	64
14	The Red Quill	71

15	Notes for a Story	76
16	The Flop House	80
17	The Peeler	83
18	Man's Best Friend	87
19	Bill the Peach	96
20	Christmas Present	102

Author's note:

The English novelist Charles Dickens was given a guided tour of several dangerous 'Rookeries' by Inspector Field, the formidable Chief Detective of Scotland Yard.

What he saw there inspired him to write some of the greatest stories of all time.

1 RED SNOW

December 20th, 1836

The snow had fallen steadily all the way through the cold, dark night, kindly providing the dead body on the cobblestones with a thick white blanket that covered it all the way from the tips of its toes to the base of the neck. But there the blanket stopped, because the body stopped too. The man's head had been pulled clean off and tossed away, coming to rest at the base of a nearby lamppost.

One of the city's registered lamp lighters had tripped over the corpse on his way down the street. These 'bringers of light' often discovered the overnight dead, not just because they were the first to walk the streets after the cock crowed, but mainly because they spent most of their time looking up, and the rest of it not watching where they were going.

Sidney Crabb had been lighting up for 20 years, during which time he'd seen most things. One morning he'd discovered a trail of limbs; whole arms and legs equally spaced on the road. That had been the local hospital wagon on its way to the crematorium with a broken axle. Every time it hit a bump or a pothole, one of the body parts had been jolted out of the vehicle. He'd discovered the driver and his mate, too, who'd realised their mistake and were making a mad dash back the way they came to collect all of the limbs before someone saw them. Another time he'd come across ten women wandering around in some sort of trance carrying a May Pole and the head of a goat. Weird stuff, but that was London, you never knew what you were going to get from one day to the other.

Sidney Crabb had discovered dead bodies before, but nothing like this one; this was nasty. He was still trembling when the Bow Street Runners arrived to investigate. This was the fifth body to be found in less than three weeks, all of which had had their heads twisted off. There were whispers in the drinking houses and the taverns. Something nasty was stalking the city, they said.

The way the bodies had been wrenched apart wasn't human. Who, or what, could do such a thing? Was it a beast? Was it something from the dark places under the city? No one knew, and no one wanted to know anything more about it. And so London started to shiver and tremble, and it had nothing to do with the plummeting temperatures. This was pure fear. The citizens of the capital began to bolt their doors, and then they turned to the one group of people they knew would do everything they could to keep them safe.

Sergeant Simeon Jewkes was ordered to lead the investigation. He'd seen the last three mutilated bodies, and when the fourth had been discovered his arm was first in the air when the Chief Inspector of the Bow Street Runners had asked for volunteers. He wasn't particularly happy or excited to be doing this, he just wanted to serve the people of the city, to protect them and make the streets he grew up on safe for everyone. And if that meant putting himself in harm's way, then so be it. Jewkes had only recently been married to his childhood sweetheart. She was a good woman called Virginia, and although she backed him to the hilt on most things, she was not best pleased when he told her that he would be working the case.

"Christmas is coming, Jewkes! And just who will bring the goose to the table and wrap the presents and warm the bed pans for the children if you are out all night searching for this monster?"

Her rants were frequent, but they were delivered without malice. Her words tumbled out because she loved him, and she was scared for him. But he knew that deep down she was proud of him, and of what he was doing.

He'd always had a strong stomach. Growing up in a street with an abattoir at one end of it and a knackers yard at the other had strengthened his resolve, and given him a pair of nostrils and a sense of smell that could filter out the very worst stench. It was just as well, he reflected as he reached the scene of the crime, because the poor individual under the snow without a head had filled his trousers during the attack, and now the snow was melting fast. Constable Tunstall, another one of the Runners that had grown up on these meanest of streets, was his 'acting second' on the case. He was a dependable sort, and he had already spoken to the people who lived and worked nearby. It was the same story as the other murders, though. No one had heard anything or seen anything, but they were terrified, and the mood was turning ugly. It wouldn't be long before the rabble was roused, and the flaming torches were lit.

Jewkes asked his men to take a look at the streets surrounding the murder scene and look for tracks in the snow. If the killer had surprised his victim then he must have been waiting for him, somewhere. Something else was beginning to bother him as well. After this sort of vicious attack, where did the murderer go? And why wasn't there more blood?

2 THE WINNING PAW

The Rat Castle is a one of London's seediest and roughest drinking dens. The worst and the best of London's criminal underclass call it their home from home, and it is often their town hall. It can be a jolly place, full of singing and dancing and everything else that makes the local priests frown and get angry on a Sunday morning, and it can also be the most frightening place in the city, if you happen to find yourself there and you do not know its rules. The Rat Castle attracts an eclectic group of patrons. You'll find pickpockets, brawlers, confidence tricksters, card sharps, whores and pug-faced enforcers here. They drink the local ale and gin, and they rub shoulders with each other quite nicely thank you very much, and they do not break the house rules. No one is allowed to practice on his neighbour whilst on Castle grounds. If you are caught tricking, stealing, trying to intimidate or abusing another, then you take a walk along the bottom of the nearest canal, carrying your dead family in your arms.

There's also another flavour of customer that enjoys the delights of the Rat Castle, but you would be hard pressed to put them into a nice, neat grouping. Fairies, Hedge Witches, members of the small people, changelings and spirits, hybrids, and beasts that long ago learned the 12 languages of the underworld drink and make merry here too.

Sitting on a large wooden chest at a table near the bar is a Bull Mastiff dog. He is almost as big as the gypsy man sitting opposite him. The Mastiff's name is Bullseye, and he is the muscle for his good friend William Sikes, a notorious housebreaker and underworld hard man, who is expected through the door at any moment. The gypsy man is known as Big Joe Rose. He is an associate of the dog's, and there is earth magic in him. He tells tales and reads palms when he is not destroying all-comers in the boxing rings and the square fighting boxes of the underworld's pugilists. The dog has his upturned paw on the table and his friend is about to read his future for him. Joe Rose is whispering to himself in a language that many in the land have forgotten already; occasionally he points at one of the dog's deep creases on its paw, and identifies it as a wealth line, or a fortune line. The dog snuffles as he drinks noisily from his specially modified tankard.

"Bullseye, you beautiful cur! See what I reads here in this, your grey and well-travelled paw? I see a pile of loot and books with you written about inside. Blimey, Bullseye! How long have you been learning to read, then? Mind you keep it from Bill, or he'll have you doing the books for him."

The dog tilts its head back and lets out a strange little howl that the gypsy and those nearby recognise as the big dog's laughter.

"Now listen here, Bullseye. I say loot and books for a reason, okay? I've heard of a nice peach of a bit of business that has actually come looking for us, for a change. Have you heard of a learned cove who writes stories and has them printed in the *Penny Dreadful*? His name is Dickens, Charles Dickens, and he's coming to the Rat Castle soon, so as to do his research for a new story. I've heard through a friend of a friend that if this person – a well-known and well-loved member of the community and dare I say, society – is taken up and held for a short time, then there would be other types that might pay to have him set free, if you know what I mean.

"It could be as sweet a piece of work for you and dearest Bill that you have had a sniff off these past months."

The dog takes another swig from his tankard, swallows, and signals to the landlord behind the bar to refresh their pots.

"That sounds just up our street, Joe. Same split as usual?"

"That sounds more than fair. You are more than a Gentleman my friend, you is a Gentle-dog. I shall see you and Bill here on the Friday coming, and you shall have the information you require."

Two tankards are placed on the wooden table between them by one of the barmaids and before she has a chance to leave the big Gypsy grabs her by the waist.

"Now little flower, should you like to hear your future and learn what road you are on?"

She laughs as she tears herself free and goes back to the bar. The dog winks at his friend and lets out another wheezy howl.

3 THE SPIRIT OF THE THREE

The man watched the house from the opposite side of the road. He could see that lots of building work and repairs had recently been carried out. There was still some scaffolding arranged about the chimney stack, and there were lots of white lumps and bumps in the garden. The man made an educated guess that underneath those snowy white humps you'd find lots of lovely new green things had just been planted. Bushes, small trees, shrubs and fresh green grass, perhaps. December was not the season to start planting, not in this country! But evidently whoever lived in this imposing old building had decided that time couldn't wait to give it a facelift and make it appear more welcoming. In five minutes' time he might discover why.

The large iron gate and its railings had been shown

some love too. They had been painted a smart grey, and the sharp tips had been crowned in gold. From his vantage point, Judas Iscariot, Thief Taker and Recovery Agent could see that a once big, dark and unloved house had been brought back to life and turned into a home. From behind the freshly-painted windows light was issuing forth, and it made Judas smile as he imagined what was going on behind them. He imagined warm rooms and roaring fires, and bells ringing in the servants quarters as people sat for dinner or guests were admitted.

He hadn't felt much warmth in this rainy, grey city since he arrived. They said this was a mild winter, but where he had come from, this level of cold would have been likened to the end of the world. He stamped his feet to dislodge the snow that had settled on his boots, checked to make sure that no horse drawn carriage was hurtling towards him, and stepped off the curb, crossing the street before pulling on the bell lever in order to announce himself to the strange businessman that had summoned him.

The butler almost ran down the path to open the gate for him. He was a rosy-cheeked fellow with creases around his eyes. After being ushered into the hall and giving the butler his long coat, hat and gloves, Judas was invited to follow the head servant down a series of corridors. He could hear laughter and music and the voices of children shouting and chasing each other. At the end of a long, well-lit corridor was a tall oak door. The butler knocked firmly, and it was opened straight away by a tall, thin man with grey hair and a long, much pulled-upon nose. He invited Judas in, and offered him a chair by the fire and a brandy. Both warmed Judas Iscariot in their own ways, and as he began to thaw out he made sure to tell his host how grateful he was.

"Mr Iscariot, your name has come to me through certain – how can I say – friends. I believe that you are a Thief Taker of some renown, and that you have never failed in any task that you have been set. Am I right in thinking that?"

Judas nodded politely.

"I am also told by these *friends* that you do not fear to tread in places where others fear to go. Into the underworld and beyond."

Judas sipped on his rather delicious brandy, and nodded once again.

"Mr Iscariot, not so long ago, I had what you might call a 'revelation', a sign from a higher power, as it were. A mirror was held up to me and I was able to see all my wrongs and my many failings. I have decided to do something about them, and that is why you are here.

"Something is stirring in the dark places. Things that do not yet have names are crossing over into this time and place, and if nothing is done about them, then our future is pretty bleak."

Judas placed his glass down on the leather-topped desk. He was suddenly very interested in what the man was saying. This was the sort of thing that he had been sent here to investigate. He reached inside his jacket pocket, removed the silver coin that he always carried with him, and began to make circular motions with his thumb on one side. The older man pretended not to notice.

"How did you come upon this information, Mr…?"

"My name is no matter, Mr Iscariot. All you need to know is that I am a friend to this city. If I told you of the messengers that brought this state of affairs to my attention then I would not be entirely surprised if you tried to have me admitted to Bedlam."

"You say messengers, Sir. As in, more than one?"

"There were three, to be precise, but I think we should focus on the here and the now if that would be agreeable to you?"

Judas shrugged.

"Right then, to the matter in hand. In two days' time, a writer by the name of Charles Dickens is planning to enter the Rookeries. I'm sure you know of them; they're a series of tenement buildings and slums that are home to the less savoury sections of our burgeoning society. Mr Dickens is planning to visit some of the local attractions in the course of researching a new book that will feature members of the underworld. One of the venues on his itinerary is a hostelry called the Rat Castle. I have reason to believe that he will come to serious harm if he is not protected there."

"What is this man to you Sir? Is he a relation?"

Judas lifted his soon to be empty glass from the table and sipped at the remaining liquor sparingly. The man noticed, immediately rising to refill Judas' glass.

"Thank you, it's excellent."

"I'm glad you approve. In answer to your question, no, Dickens is no relation to me and if we were to walk past each other in the street he would not know me. He may have some knowledge of me in the future, I hope. You never know, he might even immortalise me in one of his stories. For now, let us just agree that he is a good man in need of assistance, and that his safety will have a big difference on the lives of many unfortunates in the future. I believe that Mr Charles Dickens will bring lots of light and mirth to the people of this city in time."

He gestured towards an envelope on the desk in front of Judas.

"I have written down all of the particulars for you here, and I have arranged an introduction with a policeman who will be accompanying Mr Dickens on the night in question. Apart from your fee, I think that's everything we need to discuss."

Judas watched the plum and burgundy-coloured hues of his brandy turn to liquid fire through the diamond shaped etchings in his glass for a short while, before picking up the envelope and placing it carefully inside his jacket pocket.

"I won't take anything from you up front, sir. If I return Mr Dickens to you in one piece, hale and hearty, then we can talk of payment, but it wouldn't be right to accept anything at this stage. If there isn't anything more, sir, I think I should like to go and pay a call on the policeman you mentioned, and maybe go and find out a bit more about this Mr Dickens of yours."

"Very well, Mr Iscariot, my man will show you out. If you need anything in the meantime then please do call. Good luck, and I hope to see you soon."

Judas made his farewells, and after thanking the butler for warming his coat for him by the fire in the scullery, he was shown into the hallway, where he retrieved his hat and gloves. He turned to the servant.

"Your master is good man, and his household seems a happy one."

The butler opened the door and the moonlight barged its way in, turning the black and white tiles underfoot into shades of silver.

"Thank you for the compliment, sir, but it was no bother at all about the coat. Mr Ebenezer says that although kindness is free, it is worth more than gold."

Judas left the house and walked down the path, through the iron gate, and into danger.

4 SIKES

William Sikes, or Bill to friends and enemies alike, was bad to the core. If he'd been an apple, even the maggots would have avoided eating him. He was known to be a hard, resourceful and cruel man. Lots of his competitors had tried to bring him down, but he was still walking, talking and breathing, while they had all disappeared.

Bill had a way of disposing of things he didn't like or had no further use for. He knew people at the local ironworks and there was many a time that they left the back gates unlocked, just so that Bill could pop something into one of the brick ovens or furnaces. They didn't want to know what the fuel for the fire was and they didn't care, just as long as the usual fee was left in the rusty tin cup that hung on the wall above the pile of kindling in the workshop.

Bill was wanted by many: the Bow Street Runners, a string of private investigators and the minders and hardmen of countless city gents were all on his tail. He'd murdered many of their friends, and broken into many of their houses and warehouses. He owed them thousands of pounds in gold. They wanted him dead or alive. Alive, so that they could take their turn in making him dead.

Business had been quiet for weeks now and Bill was starting to get angry about it. It was as if he blamed the city for starving him of violence.

"That bloody dog had better have sniffed out some jobs, or else," he snarled.

A passer-by in the street saw who it was that was talking to himself, and disappeared down an alleyway. Everyone knew William Sikes round here, and they knew to avoid him. Sikes crossed the street, hiked the collars of his greatcoat up around his ears, and pulled his beaten old hat down on his head. He walked like a sailor home from the sea, rolling from side to side, always alert and ready to leap into action at the drop of a belaying pin.

The streets of Bloomsbury were quieter than normal. The killer that had taken five souls already was stalking the Rookeries as well as the better areas of the City. That's why business was quiet. The thought made him even angrier than usual, and he almost went for the old Pug that guarded the door to the Rat Castle, but common sense got the better of him just in time and he made sure to give the boxer a farthing to keep him sweet. Canvas Back Carter had been a handy fighter in his youth, but the gangs had got to him early and bribed him to take a fall. From then on he went from being a tough bantam weight to a punch-drunk drunkard. People called him Canvas Back because his back spent more time on the canvas than the soles of his boots. Ironically enough, they only called him this behind his back, because he would destroy you in a heartbeat if you crossed him. Carter pocketed the coin, touched his forelock to show his appreciation, and opened the door for Sikes. The roar and the smell rushed out to meet him, and he hurried inside.

Bullseye was sitting on the far side of the room with Gypsy Joe Rose. It was the seat and table he liked the most, with a good view of the front door so that he could slip away if needed, and nice and close to the bar. Bill saw his old and only real friend, and made his way over to him.

Bullseye and Sikes had met years ago, at one of the country fairs that came to London from time to time. Sikes was looking for someone to watch his back, and Bullseye was looking for his next fight. They were a match made in Hendon, and soon they were terrorising anyone that would let them. Bullseye was from another world, the enchanted world that occasionally overlapped with this one. He was far older than he looked, and he was very dangerous when his blood was up. He was also the only talking dog in town.

"What you got that big ugly smile on that big ugly face for, you dog?"

"Now, now then, Bill my old mate. I don't mind the ugly comment, because I'll accept I'm far from beautiful, but you know best not to call me a dog, now!"

"Sorry, Bullseye, but that killer is on the loose and it looks like it's scaring away our fortunes. The streets are deathly quiet."

"Well don't you worry about that, Bill, because I've just heard from our old mate Gypsy Joe Rose here about a nice little job that will set us up nicely for the hard winter months ahead."

"Well, have you now? Tell me more – but maybe we should head to the office first."

At this cue, the big bull mastiff jumped off his chair and trotted over to the quiet corner of the room where business was normally discussed, pulling up a seat. Sikes and Rose followed him, and soon their heads were together, whispering and nudging each other and drawing rectangles in the dust on the top of the table. One of the barmaids ambled over to see if there was anything they wanted, but she never got closer than a few feet because at the sound of her approach Bullseye whipped around and bared his long, yellow stained teeth. The dog and his partners in crime talked until they were two full candles down. They had made their plan for Mr Charles Dickens, and now it was time to drink. Bullseye gave the barmaid he had frightened an extra coin, and begged her indulgence.

As the ale flowed, neither barmaid, nor dog, nor man noticed the heap of rags on the floor behind their table stir, stretch, then get up and sidle out of the door.

5 LORD DODGER

Slick William was one of London's finest thieves, but he preferred the term 'Break's Man', because he could break into anything, anywhere. At one point in his early career he had invented another title for himself. He tried to get people to call him the 'Mirror Dancer' because he could dance his way up the side of any building, however difficult, and gracefully pick any lock. He'd announced himself as such only once, though. Proper thieves would have nothing to do with someone who gave themselves airs and graces, and they'd laughed at him openly, and ribbed him mercilessly. So he swiftly acknowledged that the old ways were the best, declared that the 'Mirror Dancer' was no more, and informed all that would listen that he should go by his earned name, which was Slick William.

He'd been working hard for the last few nights, and he'd retired to the Rat Castle to take a break and warm his meagre hams by the fire. As a small chap he did not have much of a capacity for strong ale, and after his fifth pint he'd drifted off to sleep with his head on his arms on a table at the back of the bar. One of the barmaids, who he knew moderately well, had shifted him onto one of the benches against the wall and covered him in what rags she could find.

Slick William had slept very well, and he was about to get up when he heard Bill Sikes and his mastiff muscle talking at the table nearby. What he heard made him get very excited indeed. Now, pickpockets have to move quickly – their survival depends upon it – but a Break's Man has to be able to remain very still indeed.; there are times when a good thief might only have a few minutes to scale a high wall, but then he may have to wait for a few hours before he can move on to the next part of the job. Slick William had been able to lie so still that neither Sikes or Bullseye had known he was there, and the stink of the rags that lay on him had disguised his odour to the extent that even Bullseye's famous sniffing power had not discovered him. So he heard all about Charles Dickens, the kidnapping plot, and the hundreds of pounds that they thought they might be able to squeeze out of his posh friends. Once they had gone, and the coast was clear, Slick William slipped away and ran like his life depended on it to the person to whom he owed fealty, Lord Dodger.

Slick William exited the Rat Castle by the rear

door, which was actually a heavy curtain weighed down with bricks to stop it flapping and letting in the cold night air. Once across the road, he looked around to make sure that he hadn't grown an extra shadow and seeing that he was all alone, he shinned up a pipe that was clinging to the side of a building for dear life. Reaching the top, he pulled himself up and onto the roof and sat there for a minute to take another look at the street below. In his business there was only safe, there was no sorry.

After a few minutes he stood up and stretched, scratched his armpit and had a good smell of his clothes. He was nearly sick. He smelled rancid, but he didn't have time to bathe or change his clothes. He'd be sure to tell Lord Dodger that he had suffered to bring this piece of prime knowledge to him, and just had to hope that he wasn't thrown out of court for humming as badly as he did right then. Slick William set off at a jog up here on the rooftops, or the Moonlit Roads as the criminal classes referred to them; he didn't have to dodge any carts or hide from the Bow Street Runners, so he was able to fly along.

Occasionally he would see something or hear something and skid to a halt. When he did have to stop like this, he quickly faded into the nearest shadow to watch and wait. More often than not the disturbance would be a mangy cat or a startled pigeon, but there had been rumours that something ungodly was also moving around up here. Once he was sure that the noise didn't belong to something nasty he set off again.

Most of the buildings in the Rookeries were only spitting distance from each other but here and there, there were a few big gaps. So long planks of wood had been stolen from the barges on the nearby canals, and they had been hidden away on the rooftops to be used as bridges between buildings in times of need.

He was halfway across one of these bridges when he saw something moving out of the corner of his eye. It wasn't very big, but it was moving fast, and it was moving straight towards him.

Fear makes people do one of two things straight away – either they run like the Devil, or they drop to their knees and start hoping that God will show up. Slick William was across that plank of wood and pulling it across the gap and away from whatever it was that was coming for him in a flash. And then he was clattering across the rooftops, sending loose slates down onto the streets below like black squares of falling night. He knew better than to look behind him, that was the way they always caught you. 'Look back to gloat, and off the rooftops you float', was what the clever thieves said.

Slick William couldn't write his own name, but he was smart in his own way, and he was almost there; the last thing he was going to do was to look over his shoulder or slip. Which is exactly what he did, exactly when he didn't want to do it. Water had collected in a pool at the side of a chimney stack, and over time the water had found its way through to the rooms below. The roof itself had become spongy, and as he reached it, Slick William put his foot right through it. He tumbled forward, rolled over twice and then threw himself through the nearest glass skylight.

He landed on one of the sorting tables. There were lots of sorting tables in Lord Dodger's court. Sorting tables for stolen goods, sorting tables for watches, wallets, notebooks, books, rings and bracelets and silver boxes. And a sorting table for silk scarves and handkerchiefs. Slick William crashed through the roof and missed the table full of the fragile and most expensive objects, coming down to earth with a muffled thump. The fighting coves that Lord Dodger employed to keep the peace were all over him in an instant. They thought that he must be a member of another gang come to make mischief, but when they saw who it was they groaned.

"It's only Slick William, Lord Dodger! And Christ, he does smell bad," said one.

Half an hour later, he was regaling the King of the Pickpockets with his story and apologising, over and over again for his appearance. Lord Dodger had been King for many years, and he had learned how to listen and how to rule. He'd been described as tall on the handbills that were circulated by the Runners when they'd asked for any information that would help apprehend him. His dark hair was as black as his beaten old hat; if you saw him before the candles had been lit of an evening you might have thought that he was wearing a big hood instead. His court was huge. The loft space of two warehouses had been combined to make one huge room, and this was from where Lord Dodger ruled his empire. No criminal act in the Rookeries was unknown to him or his spies, and he demanded his tribute for each and every one of them. He always wore a big starched collar, too; it made him look a bit like the Mad Hatter. This ruler drank no tea, though; he drank wine, and lots of it.

Once Slick William had told his tale, been paid for his endeavours and advised to take a bath or two, Lord Dodger sent a handful of his men into the streets to see if anyone had heard anything about this visit to the Rookeries by Dickens, or about this, shadowy creature that was haunting the rooftops at night.

6 THE ROOKERY

Judas was up early that morning. He'd shaved in a bowl of steaming hot water brought up to his room by the youngest maid of the house. She was a lovely girl and very helpful. He'd forgotten to button his shirt when she entered the room, and she had nearly dropped the hot water on to the rug in the middle of his room. The scar on his stomach was an angry red and puckered purple, and although he had forgotten that he wore it, it was still fairly nasty to behold. The thin scar around his neck, the one caused by the noose that he himself had tied to the branch of the tree in the olive grove, had faded and turned white to the extent that it provoked only the slightest of reactions in those who saw it.

God had decided that suicide was not a door that

Judas would ever pass through. Do good, fight evil in all its forms, and protect the weak. These were just some of the words that the Almighty had poured into him that night. He'd made Judas immortal, and told him that the road ahead was long – very long. There would be no easy reprieve for him. Judas must make amends for betraying his son.

After shaving he'd taken breakfast in one of the chop houses nearby. The coffee they served was awful, while the other thing that the locals drank, a variant of tea, was just heated water with twice-strained leaves. Having drunk proper tea in China, and coffee in the Levant, he knew what he was talking about on both counts, and these offerings were as far from the real thing as he was from the real places they came from. The food, though, was good, and it filled his stomach and delivered some much-needed warmth to his cold limbs.

It would take time, but he might get used to this damp place despite its constantly bad weather. There was something so wild and vibrant about the city. The moment he had stepped off the boat and set foot on land, he felt the power of the ages coursing through him. This England, this old Albion, had secrets and ancient lore. And where magic is strong, evil grows, which after all, was what he had been sent here to find.

Judas paid the keeper of the house and thanked her for her hospitality. She took his money gladly, and then he set off to meet with the other men whose task it was to protect the man whom his client was so concerned about – Charles Dickens.

Number 4, Whitehall Place, was the address he had been told to find by the old gentleman, but when Judas arrived, he couldn't find the front door. So he stopped a young constable in the street and asked, politely, where he could find Inspector Field of the Metropolitan Police. The constable had smiled, and taken Judas to the back of Whitehall Place to a location called Scotland Yard. The rear door to 4 Whitehall Place had been chosen as the main entrance for the Met's Headquarters, and people were just starting to get used to calling the place where the coppers were based Scotland Yard.

Judas entered, feeling a strange surge of energy as he did so. He liked what he saw. There were lots of men, women and boys racing around the entrance hall, shouting at each other, delivering post and what looked like prisoners and criminals to various corners of the building. At the reception point stood a desk sergeant wearing a pair of massive sideburns. Every time he turned his head he tempted fate; his handlebars were coated in wax and the bare lamps on the walls were naked flames. If he strayed too closely his whole head would have gone up like a bonfire.

Judas waited patiently in line. He had managed to secure a seat at the back of the hallway so that he could observe the comings and the goings of the mighty Metropolitan Police Force. It was already feared and revered in equal measure, and the man that cracked the whip the hardest was the man he had been sent here to speak with. Judas was happy to sit and wait. He took out his silver coin, one of the 30 that he was cursed to keep, and rubbed at it. The noise faded and he closed his eyes. He dreamed of angels, and one big angel in particular.

He was only a short time in the world of dreams when he was shaken by the shoulder by the desk sergeant. In the real world, the realm of men and punctuality, an hour had passed.

"Mr Iscariot, Sir? Inspector Field is ready to see you, Sir. Take the stairs to the top floor and then ask for the Inspector."

Judas nodded to the sergeant in thanks, then made his way to the stairs at the back of the building. His footsteps echoed on the highly polished wooden steps, and as he ascended he stared into the faces of many of the brave men and women of the force that had died in the service of law and order. Their pictures and portraits looked out from the walls, and every one of them had pride and purpose written in the stories of their faces. Judas hoped that one day someone might look on his face and think that he was worth remembering – for all the right reasons, this time. When he reached the top of the stairs he didn't need to ask for the Inspector, because he could hear him. Someone was getting a dressing down, and Judas was happy that he wasn't on the receiving end of it.

Judas waited for the shouting to stop and for the poor individual who had just been given a professional warning to exit the office, then he made his way along the corridor and tapped on the door.

"Come!" said a booming voice.

Judas opened the door and stepped inside.

"Inspector Field, my name is Judas Iscariot. I have a letter from a mutual friend for you."

Judas removed the pristine white envelope from his jacket pocket and handed it over to the man behind the desk. As he read it, Judas had a chance to observe him. He must have been at least six foot four and a good 14 stones in weight, with hands that had brushed a few chins in their time. Smartly dressed, and clearly in possession of physical power, he looked to Judas like a leader by example, and no one-trick-pony.

Inspector Field read the letter of introduction twice. Judas could see his eyes scanning the page up and down, making sure not to miss an inference here, or a suggestion there. After he had finished reading, he folded it neatly back in half, inserted it back inside the envelope, and placed it on the desk in front of him.

"Please sit down, Mr Iscariot. The chair by the fire, if you please."

Judas crossed the room and sat down as requested at a fire that was small, but welcome. The Inspector waited for him to settle, then stood up and walked around the desk, making himself comfortable in the chair on the other side of the fire, so that he was looking directly into Judas' eyes.

"Our mutual friend has had some sort of a revelation of late. A short while ago you'd have had trouble getting a smile out of him, yet now he wants to help every single one of London's children. Half the moneylenders in the city are pulling their hair out because he's stopped helping people out of business and more of them into it. He's throwing grants and bursaries about like confetti, too. Now don't get me wrong, I'd rather he was like this than the way he was before, but he does like to… meddle. And that, I think, is what brings you to my door, Mr Iscariot. Apparently you have been retained by our friend to look after Mr Charles Dickens tonight.

"From what I have heard of you through my men on the street, you are dependable and resourceful, and handy when things get tight. Would that be a fair assessment of your character?"

"I have walked the darker side of the streets in many cities, Inspector. I try to do good wherever I can with the tools at my disposal."

The Inspector raised his eyebrows.

"Well, the places we are going to visit tonight are by far the worst and most dangerous that this fair city has to offer. The streets and the lanes of the Rookeries of St Giles, Jacob's Island and Rat Castle are nasty places; a man might get lost in there and never reappear. The canals are full of bodies, and the rats grow fat on them. I have confidence in my men because they know these streets; many of them are local to the area. I can depend on them not to run at the first sign of trouble, but can I trust you to stand if things get ugly, Mr Iscariot?"

"Inspector, may I show you something?"

"If it will argue your case and persuade me to let you follow me and Mr Dickens into the black, beating heart of the East End of London, show away."

Judas stood up and removed his jacket. Then he unbuttoned his shirt and pulled it open to reveal his scars.

The old and experienced policeman had seen scars and wounds before; he'd seen the very limits of human depravity. He was not shocked. Judas hadn't meant him to be.

"I will not bother you with the stories behind many of my scars, nor will I go into depth about the big one on my stomach and the one around my neck. I ran away from something once, long ago, and I was punished, savagely and brutally. I have never ever run away from anything ever since. You can rely on me, Inspector, I'm not in the habit of betraying anyone anymore."

Judas did up his shirt and jacket, and sat back down.

The Inspector narrowed his eyes and made a steeple with his fingers. He stared for a short while and Judas got the feeling that he must be trying to read his soul from behind those bushy eyebrows. Good luck finding that, he thought.

"Meet me at the Beaux Belles public house on the corner of Ivy Street in Bloomsbury at 10 o'clock, Mr Iscariot. I will introduce you to Mr Dickens, and then I shall share the plan for our little excursion with you. We won't be travelling far and wide, though. There will be six of us in total: myself, Mr Dickens and his assistant, two armed men, and you, of course. I have a division of local constables on standby and they will swarm into action on my whistle blast if needs be. Dress warmly, and bring whatever protection you think fit. Good day, sir."

Inspector Field stood up and marched back to his desk, buried his head in the mountains of paperwork on it and didn't look up from the horror stories in front of him as Judas left. As far as interviews had gone, this one had been short and sharp, just the way Judas liked them to be. He stepped out into the declining light of day and wondered to himself what exactly a dingy, dirty yard in London had to do with Scotland.

7 TURN AND TURN ABOUT

The pretty flower had nine petals. They were whiter than white, and they felt soft to the touch. The centre of the flower was yellow, and it reminded him of the sun, so he pressed the tip of his thumb into it, as hard as he could possibly press, because he wanted to blind the sun, because he hated it so. But when the sun died in his hands, so did the flower, and that made him very angry indeed. A pigeon flew into the abandoned attic that he called home through the biggest of the many holes in his roof, and settled on one of the rafters. It flapped its wings once more and dislodged a scuttle's worth of dust. The boy watched the motes fall. Some of the dust landed on the head of the man propped up against the far wall. He was still out cold, and his head was lolling to one side. Dribble from his open mouth had connected his chin to his chest with a slither of white static lightning. Or so the boy imagined. He threw a rock at the pigeon and it flew away.

The flapping of its escaping wings caused the man to wake. His eyes opened and there was more than just a hint of madness and panic in them. He scanned the room, not knowing where he was, looking for something to link him back to his own world, but he didn't find anything. That was when the boy decided to speak.

"Now, now, petal. Would you like some *more*?" said the boy.

His voice was sweet and soft – puberty had not robbed him of its purity yet – but the man heard only evil, and the terror he felt made him panic. There was a broken window on the far side of the room. It had no panes of glass, and only a partial frame. The man guessed what the view from that window would be, and his mind was already processing just how far he was from a potential escape route. But then the boy stepped out of the darkness he had been sitting in and walked over to him.

"I was never afraid to ask for more. But you are. What's wrong? Not hungry?"

The man stood up. He towered over the boy, but he was absolutely terrified. He kicked and punched him, but the boy was immovable. Then, as if tiring of his plaything, the boy grabbed hold him, and threw him across the room. When the man came to again, the little boy's hands were around his neck. They shouldn't have been able to encircle it, let alone exert the immense pressure he was feeling from them. The boy started to sing a song. Something about 'buying some wonderful flowers'. And then he began to twist the man's head off.

"Twist and twist and twist! Please, sir, can I have some more?"

The man blacked out after the first turn, and was dead by the second.

Once he'd finished twisting, and the man's head had been pulled from his body, the boy stood up and carried body and head across the dusty room until he was standing directly underneath the skylight in the roof. Then, he jumped. One second he was in the garret, the next he was on the rooftop. It was a leap that no human could have ever made. Unless, of course, its body was being shared with a malevolent demon set on causing carnage and spreading despair and sorrow.

From this vantage point, the demon could see the slums for miles around. It could smell the people and the foul stench of the canals and the rotting horseflesh in the streets, and it liked it – what demon wouldn't? It was beginning to get accustomed to the boy's body now, which was a shame, because soon it would have to return to the underworld and pay for breaking the rules.

What was one more broken rule though, hey? thought the demon.

It started to cackle to itself, before casually tossing

the dead body and head into the canal below.

"Please, sir, can I have some more? Can I have some more people's heads to twist?"

8 LITTLEWING

Judas made his way back to the lodging house through streets that fairly hummed with humanity. He'd travelled through big cities before. Some of them left him breathless with their beauty, while some, like London, left him breathless because of the smog, smoke and the press of the millions that lived there. On the streets, bullocks and oxen that appeared to Judas to have taken the wrong turn and left the countryside by mistake, pulled their carts through the mud and the puddles left behind by the last rain shower. Little children ran this way and that, daring each other to scamper between the legs of stationary horses and everywhere, the noise of the living assaulted him. His boots were filthy, so he used the scraper at the front door to the building to remove as much dirt and slime as he could. He needn't have bothered, because one of the maids was already stationed at the door to take them away and have them cleaned properly.

He heard the murmur of the other lodgers chatting to each other in the smoking room as he climbed the stairs. He'd never been a smoker of anything, and he thought the huge curved pipes that the average London gentleman sucked and puffed on were odd-looking objects. The time that they spent grounding the old, dead flakes out of the pipe itself with small hand-made tools made him shake his head in disbelief, too.

His room was at the top of the house. He'd asked for it especially. He needed to be somewhere where he could hear himself think. He reached out for the highly polished brass doorknob and he was about to enclose it in his hand and turn it when he felt the magic. He stopped and took a few steps back. He didn't like surprises, particularly the sort that could enter his room without using the stairs.

"You're not going to stand out there all day are you, Deceiver? I've had to fly very hard to get here and I'd like to get back sharpish. Come on in, I won't bite."

Judas thought he recognised the voice, and he opened the door quickly and stepped inside.

Angels don't like sleeping on flat surfaces. They tuck their wings back, then sort of shuffle backwards and lean into them, allowing their wings to become a sort of feathered hammock. Judas had watched many of them do it over the years. Angels were incredibly powerful, and yet they were graceful, even when they were angry and ripping their enemies apart in the heat of battle. Style was everything.

"Good morrow to you Judas, betrayer of the God child and King of the Deceivers.

"I am called Littlewing, for obvious reasons, a messenger angel from the fourth level of the Host. I bring you tidings from the Archangel Michael, and a message from him."

Judas made sure that the door to his room was fully closed, then removed his long coat and hung it up in the bare wardrobe that stood against the wall.

"Is that what they're calling me up there in the City of the Heavens, Littlewing – 'the Deceiver'? Sounds very grand and massively pompous, but I suppose you must get bored up there, flying around and making sure the gardens are nice and tidy."

The angel moved so fast that Judas was standing upright one second and then found himself crumpled up and stuck in the bottom of the wardrobe the next.

"I may only be a messenger, Judas Iscariot, killer of the son of the One, but I am still one of the Host. As such, if you speak ill of the Host or our gardening prowess, I will pull your arms off, okay? Now get out of that stupid cabinet and take a seat. I have much to tell you."

Judas did as he was told and he hoped that the sound of the scuffle had not been heard downstairs. If anyone were to investigate it and they were to find a real, living and breathing angel in his room taking tea with him, then he would be packing his bag and getting out of town faster than he had done in Berlin. Littlewing was a little on the small side for an angel, but he was still a good head and shoulders taller than Judas. Once they had both taken a seat and Judas had gone through the motions of making a small pot of tea, Littlewing passed on his messages.

"There has been some infighting in the Host. Alliances have been made and it looks like there will be another purge. The Archangel thinks that there are still some of the Morningstar's followers in the City of the Heavens.

"Things are on edge up there, Judas. And, in the midst of all of this unrest and uncertainty, Lucifer has been making trouble."

Judas poured the tea and placed a cup and saucer in front of Littlewing. The angel smiled, and cocked his head to one side like a bird. Angels find a lot of the things that 'his creations' do rather quirky and odd, but they are touched by random acts of kindness. They spend all of their time in service to the Archangels and to 'Him', always giving and sacrificing, so that when someone does something for them, they notice, and they are moved. Littlewing tried the tea.

"Not the best I have ever tasted, Judas, but very welcome. I thank you."

"It's my pleasure, you've come a long way. Tell me, why should this purge be of interest to me?"

"The Morningstar has been planning something for a while now, Judas. We hear rumblings of it, and occasionally we get lucky and catch one of his followers, then, after Michael has finished interrogating them, we can normally stop whatever it was that the Lord of the Fallen was trying to make happen. So far, so good. But every now and again something slips through the net and we lose track of it. We're pretty sure that a demon has crossed over into this realm and hidden itself in the city and is doing what demons normally do – which is a lot of killing."

"Fantastic! I've only been in this city for a short while and now I have some rancid second-rate demon to deal with. Do you have a name? It's normally handy to have that if you want to get rid of it quickly."

The angel picked up his cup and saucer again and drank what remained of his tea, then it replaced the empty cup and saucer on the table once more.

"We think that it may be called Azarock, but we're not sure. It will have almost certainly have possessed a good, innocent soul already, and is able to walk through the streets without causing any alarm.

"If you come across it and you fight, this might come in handy."

Littlewing reached inside his tunic and produced a small knife. It had a dull blade and a short wooden handle and looked nothing like a demon-killing weapon at all. Judas was more than a little underwhelmed.

"What am I supposed to do with that?" he said.

The angel smiled again and handed the knife over to him.

"When you need it most it will be ready, never fear. But if the knife fails, you can always rip the demon's soul out from its host's body and then eat it; that would also do the trick."

Littlewing stood up and moved to the small open window. He stood in front of it and whispered something that Judas could not hear. Then with one powerful thrust, the angel passed through the panes of glass and the wooden frame without breaking either, shooting up into the dark night sky and disappearing into the void.

Judas checked the window frame for damage but there was none. He would have to learn that spell. There had been countless times in the past where he had needed to clamber through a small space without making a lot of noise and failed – miserably. Never mind that now, he had a promising young writer to protect and if the clock on the mantle was right he had better start getting himself and his kit together. It was only when he was very near the meeting place that he remembered that he had left the knife on the desk in his room.

9 DICKENS

The Beaux Belles was a well-kept public house in the better part of Bloomsbury. The owners were two jolly ladies who had fallen in love with all things French. Their father had named the pub The Bow Bells as an homage to his cockney roots, but his darling girls had whipped the sign off and replaced it with the current one before his bones were cold. They were well-liked and they ran a straight house. Their regulars were not angels – far from it –but they liked a place where they could relax and not worry about getting stabbed in the back or poisoned with the pox. The 'Belles' was neutral ground, and it welcomed one and all, which was why Inspector Field had chosen it to run through his plan for their tour of the Rookeries.

The crowd was four-deep at the bar when Judas entered. A small grey cloud of tobacco smoke floated above the heads of the drinkers and a young woman stood on an upturned barrel in the corner, singing a song so sweetly that it brought a tear to the eyes of the hardest souls there. Behind her, and in front of the pub's open fire, was a small round table, and this was where Inspector Field had set up his briefing room.

Judas made his way through the crowd, patting himself down to make sure that no pickpocket had relieved him of any of his property. Inspector Field noticed the move and smiled.

"Mr Iscariot, may I present Mr Charles Dickens, his assistant Mr Grimes and constables Benjamin and Tunstall.

"Mr Iscariot comes highly recommended, Mr Dickens. He is a resourceful and competent agent and will be operating as your bodyguard this evening."

Judas shook hands with each man, as was the custom in England. The two constables looked fit and had a familiar quietly strong look about them. They would not back down in a fight; good men to have on your side. Mr Grimes meanwhile was a short, barrel-chested chap. He was an assistant and a servant. You could tell that immediately by his body language and positional sense. He hung back, standing a little to one side, ready to step in and provide help even before his master knew that it was needed. He had a boxer's nose, and his weight was balanced on the balls of his feet, which normally indicated that he was a proper fighter to boot.

He looked a tough nut, too, thought Judas.

Then, there was Mr Charles Dickens, the man he must keep alive tonight. Dickens was about the same height as Judas, dressed smartly, with thick dark hair and a beard that was trying to behave and point downwards but had decided to go wild at the last moment. His eyes were clear and intelligent, and Judas could see that he was recording every detail of their meeting. The people in the bar, the faces of the dogs and the sounds and smells of the London – he clearly wanted to dive into everything he encountered, and then immortalise it all in print.

A good policeman sees the world in many of the same ways as a writer, and Inspector Field was evidently one such man; on duty all of the time, looking for danger, watching to see that no harm be done, anticipating and planning for every alternative.

When Judas looked around the table he was struck by just how unusual this whole scenario was. Here he stood, hired by an old businessman that had undergone some sort of life changing experience to protect a young writer during a trip into the bad streets of the slums and the Rookeries of London. Inspector Field interrupted his thoughts.

"Would you care for a drink, sir, before we begin?"

"Something warm and wet would not go amiss, Inspector."

The Inspector nodded to Constable Tunstall; the young policeman excused himself politely and then made his way to the bar. He returned a short while later with a pint of warmed punch and handed it to Judas. It smelled wonderful, and warmed him immediately. The Inspector waited a few moments to allow everyone to get comfortable before reaching inside his overcoat and removing a folded piece of paper from his inside pocket. He flattened it out on the top of the table, and as one, the group leaned in. But before the Inspector could start to tell them about the details of his plan, Charles Dickens had a few words of his own to offer.

"Gentlemen, before we begin, might I just say that I am honoured and reassured by your presence and I thank you for it, wholeheartedly. To have London's finest police Inspector and his good men alongside me, and you, Mr Iscariot, I shall be safer in your hands and in these dangerous and rough streets than if I were at home and beside my own fire. Thank you, gentleman, thank you very much."

Inspector Field acknowledged him with a nod.

"You are too kind, Mr Dickens, we shall do our best to show you what you want to see in safety. Shall we begin?"

The Inspector started his briefing and talked without interruption for the next five minutes. It was testament to his skill and organisational acumen that at the end of it, each man knew where he would start and where he would finish, and the cut-out points where they should rally if they were attacked or found themselves in harm's way. The civilians, Dickens and Grimes, were given police whistles and told how many blasts they should sound to call for assistance, and lastly what their marching order should be. Inspector Field would lead, followed by PC Tunstall, then Grimes and Dickens, Judas and in the rear, PC Benjamin.

The Belles had filled up to capacity whilst they had been familiarising themselves with the plan, and there was now a heaving, swaying wall of people in the bar. They finished their drinks and checked the map for the seventh time before slipping out of the rear door and heading south towards the maze of dark streets where Charles Dickens hoped to find inspiration for his novels.

The streets were still noisy and full of people. There were those that were just finishing for the day after long, long hours of graft and grime, and then there were the night people, who were just stirring and stretching and easing themselves into the dark hours like cats.

Judas watched Dickens closely. He was not short of courage, that much was obvious. He held his head high and walked with purpose. Judas wondered what he would be like if he found himself on his own and fighting for his life. Hopefully that scenario would not play out tonight.

Inspector Field and his constables, Dickens, Grimes and Judas crossed the street and turned to their left. Bloomsbury was behind them now, and it was as if some giant hand had reached down from the heavens and extinguished all of the light. They arrived at the Rookeries, and entered the dark quarter.

10 WATCHING THE WATCHERS

The boy's body would fail completely soon, and then the demon Azarock would have to return whence it came. Possession takes its toll on both the possessed and the possessor, after all. One more night of feeding and amusement, then back to the City of Flames. The demon climbed down from the garret under the eaves using the rickety walkways and the rotten timbers that kept the buildings of the slums from toppling over as ladders. When he reached the ground, he stopped, and listened to the noises of the night. Away to the left, the canal gurgled, and the empty barges obeyed the tides and thumped at its sides again and again. Nearby, what sounded like a rat plopped into the dirty black mirror that was the dank and brackish water of the Thames, while in the distance someone screeched with mirth.

The demon made the boy's body sit down against the wall, and waited. Waifs and strays always came this way. The little boys and girls, the innocents and the orphans. They thought that if they avoided the busy streets hereabouts then they would not come to the attention of the wrong sort and be snatched up and taken away to dark places.

He hears them coming from far away. The moon has hardly moved at all and the night is oh so young. Two creatures have entered the street from the far end. One smells of dog and the other of rum and broken noses. They saunter along the other side of the street. Their manner tells the demon all he wishes to know in an instant. These two are rough and mean, full to the brim with anger, arrogance and cruelty. They will fill Azarock up nicely. They are fine specimens indeed. It hops from foot to foot, getting excited. Now that the two figures are closer, he can see that the one that smells of dog is actually a dog. It is one of the enchanted creatures from the world that overlaps with this one. It is very big, almost the size of a small bear, and the man beside it has wide shoulders; there is plenty of meat on his bones. The demon detaches itself from the wall and starts to follow the two creatures from a safe distance, listening intently to their conversation, and liking what it is hearing.

"Well now, Bullseye, tonight is the night! This Dickens cove is paying us poor street folk a visit, and we, my friend, will help him to see some very interesting sights."

"Yes Bill, that we shall, he may even decide to stay a while and enjoy our hospitality."

"That's right, Bullseye, he'll stay all right, whether he wants to or not."

"Your mate over at the Scotland Yard says there will be six of them then, Bill?"

"That's right. Inspector Field himself, a couple of his men as guard for this Dickens, and possibly the writer's man too. Six in total. We just have to split them up, then pick our man up, and it's as good as guineas in your pocket. Them that has pockets, that is, Bullseye; them that as wears clothes."

"You are a funny gentleman, you know that, Bill. You should be walking the boards and telling your jokes and funny stories. Now let's get a move on, shall we? Gypsy Joe Rose says that the party in question will be coming into the Rookeries from the Bloomsbury side, and I know just where we can sit and wait for them."

The two creatures continue to snipe at each other in a friendly way as they walk along together, and the demon gets hungrier and hungrier as it follows.

You could twist those fine necks straight off, but why have two, when you could have six necks instead, it thinks to itself.

11 FRIGHT THEN FLIGHT

Inspector Field stood to one side to allow a horse-drawn cart to move past him in the lane. The rest of the party followed suit. Then when the lane was empty once again, they set off for the Rat Castle.

So far this evening they had been to two locations that had caused Mr Charles Dickens to reach for his third notebook. Dickens seemed to find something of interest in the smallest thing. A small, sickly-looking boy with a crutch being carried through a crowd on the shoulder of his older brother was worth 4 pages alone. Each time he filled a page it was hurriedly grasped by Mr Grimes, and into the leather satchel around his neck it went. Judas smiled, surprised at how much Dickens saw, and how quickly. The Rat Castle was the last place on the list. Only once that evening had Judas needed to step forward and intervene on Dickens' behalf. A rather tipsy-looking little Trollope had fallen into his arms and whilst Dickens was trying to steady her she was rifling through his jacket pockets. No harm was done, and nothing was stolen. Judas had tipped the girl a coin and wished her better luck next time.

Constables Tunstall and Benjamin had both done their jobs well. If there had been any possible trouble at the head or the back of the group, Judas had not seen it. Inspector Field stopped at the end of the lane and carefully scanned the scene in front of them. He made a mental note of how many doorways had people in them, the number of cabs, and how many ladies of the night were promenading under sputtering gas lamps. Once he was happy with the lay of the land he beckoned for Tunstall to come to him. Field whispered something to the young policeman, who walked on to the street and approached the doorman of the Rat Castle. Tunstall tipped his bowler hat to the man and they spoke quickly. Some money changed hands, hats were tipped once again, and then they were admitted. One hour later, Dickens had used up all of his remaining notebooks and asked to borrow Inspector Field's own pad. He was politely refused, and the Inspector had decided that the absence of any further pages to scribble upon might suggest it could be a good time to call it a night. Dickens pleaded with the group to go on at first, but came to his senses. Inspector Field led them out, they crossed back over the street, and turned into the lane they had come up only an hour before.

Judas stayed close to Dickens, who was in a state of high excitement. He was glad that he had done so, because the moment they were all in the lane something came hurtling out of the darkness and plucked poor Grimes into the air before disappearing. They heard Grimes screaming, but could not see him to rush to his aid.

Seconds after the screaming had stopped, a flurry of pages dropped out of the sky above them. They were the notes that Dickens had written. Inspector Field was slow to react; he'd never seen or experienced anything like this, he was used to looking his enemy in the eye. Judas saw the confusion writ large on his face and snatched the police whistle from Dickens, giving the three short blasts that would alert the back-up force and guide them to their current position.

Judas grabbed hold of Dickens, pushed him back against the wall, and stood guard in front of him. He could feel the other man's breath on the back of his neck. But if Dickens was afraid now, then what he heard next tipped him over the edge into abject terror.

"Please, sir, can I have some more...?"

The voice that reached out to them from the darkness was too small, and too light. It couldn't possibly belong to a monster or anything capable of picking up a grown man and carrying him away. Inspector Field and his constables blew their whistles, and from the end of the lane came a sound that could have been a reply. Judas had been in many fights and skirmishes, though, and he had learned never to trust the sounds of the night. That high piping sound might be anything. Unfortunately, Field forgot his own experience in his haste to gain strength in numbers. In the confusion he made an error of judgement and ran towards the noise, taking his constables with him.

Judas saw in an instant what their attacker wanted to achieve. Whatever the creature was, it knew how to fight, and it had reduced their larger force to something much more easily managed. Judas turned around and took Dickens by the shoulders.

"We have to get back to the Rat Castle, Mr Dickens, where there is light and noise we are safe. Anything can happen in these quiet and empty streets, and if no eye sees it, then no voice can send for help and we shall be on our own. Come, Mr Dickens, have courage now; we may outsmart this thing yet!"

Judas pulled Dickens back along the lane towards the Rat Castle. They had nearly reached the end, and were within hailing distance of the street, when something hit Judas so hard in the chest that it lifted him off his feet and sent him flying back down the lane. The blow would have killed any normal man. But Judas was far from normal. Because he had committed the crime of all crimes, God had decided to send him out into the world to do battle with evil wherever he found it for however long he deemed necessary. Judas was not impervious to pain, but he was immortal, until told otherwise.

So he got back up and he attacked. Dickens was being carried over a wall by what looked like a child.

He wasn't fighting back, so Judas presumed that he must be unconscious. He vaulted over the wall after their attacker, and when he landed on the other side he saw his adversary clearly. It was a male child, no more than ten years of age. Blonde haired, blue eyed, and thin, as all children who live on bleak streets are. Judas sized up his opponent, taking nothing for granted. The child could not stand still. It shifted its weight from foot to foot and its neck flicked sideways, almost touching a shoulder with the flat of its ear.

It was, without question, possessed by something that should not be roaming these streets.

Was the demon on holiday? Or had it slipped into this world without permission from its lord and master, thought Judas as he watched it move back and forth. Littlewing had said that it was only a minor demon, and he probably knew its name, both of which were elements that stood in his favour. The scar on his stomach began to throb and itch.

"A bit late to sound the alarm, isn't it?"

Judas made his move.

"Put him down now, little demon, and try me instead."

"Can I? That sounds most agreeable."

The demon placed the unconscious body of Dickens down on the muddy ground beside him and stepped away from it. Dickens moaned, and that made Judas very happy indeed. If you can call out in pain then you are not dead, at least not yet.

"You must be a child of the City of Flames, then?

A lower-order demon by the sound of it."

Azarock gurgled, and the tongue that he had not yet got used to using in the boy's mouth made a horrid clicking sound.

"Maybe I am, maybe I'm not. You are a stranger here too are you not, Mr 'policeman'?"

Judas took one step back. Not out of fear, but because he wanted this demon or whatever it was away from Dickens and into the open ground, so that if things got really out of hand, and buildings started coming down, at least the man would live.

"You're right. I'm from a place that I think you know well. A place of beginnings and power. You know of where I speak, don't you? The place where the light was shaped and sent out into the world to undo your master's work. Oh, and, just for the record, I'm not a 'policeman'. But I'm warming to the task."

The demon sensed that something was amiss, and because it was stupid and only from the third Level in the City of Flames, it attacked straight away. It crossed the space between them at an incredible speed, but experience always outsmarts impatience, and Judas calmly swatted the child into the nearby canal. The demon surfaced. Its form, clothed in the body of the boy, still had enough of its power to make the water boil around it. It climbed up the moss-covered walls of the disused canal, and when it had clambered out of the seething water, it searched the night for its enemy. Judas was not hiding, and the two of them came together again and again in the shadow of a building that should have given up standing many years ago. The shock of the blows that they gave and received made old cracked bricks fall, and the old woodlouse-riven timbers crash down around them. Judas was struck on the head with an iron hoop that had once belonged to a hogshead barrel. But he kept going. There was no other option for him.

The demon was starting to get tired, and Judas moved in for the kill.

Charles Dickens rolled over onto his back and cried out into the night. He had suffered a broken rib, and the pain of movement had brought him swimming back up into the bright light of consciousness. He remembered a little boy flying over the wall like a spectre dressed in black, like a ghastly vision from some Hellish nightmare. Then the dark figure had smashed him into the wall, and he had fallen.

He looked around through a haze of pain. He was in some sort of open space, there were canal boats and jetties, some loading platforms and a huddle of derelict warehouses surrounded by even more dark buildings.

Something was happening in front of him. Two figures were fighting. One was the little boy he had seen, and the other was the man who was here to protect him. The battle was savage and unforgiving. Charles Dickens was no coward, he would fight if he thought he could help, but this encounter was something entirely different. He could do nothing to help, so he did what he had been instructed to do by Inspector Field earlier that evening at the Beaux Belles, and he ran. He ran like the very devil himself was after him.

Judas saw him leave out of the corner of his eye. The demon was fading fast. His blows were getting softer and weaker, and he knew that it was only a matter of time, now. He smashed the boy down onto the ground, then picked him up and threw him as hard as he could at the brick wall of the building nearby. The demon bounced off it and it did not get up again. The fight was over.

Judas walked over to the body. He was just about to pick it up so that he could take it to a priest and have him remove the demon, when the wall in front of him collapsed, burying him in a thunderstorm of rubble.

12 GOOD BAD LUCK

Sikes and Bullseye had been waiting patiently in a hovel that one of their associates called home. That associate was doing five years in Pentonville, so it was unlikely that they would be disturbed. There was a small fire in the hearth, and a couple of bottles of watered-down brandy. It was Sikes who saw Inspector Field charging down the street outside, followed by what looked like a whole division of police officers. They were all whistling like mad and shouting loud enough to wake the dead. Something had gone wrong and they were tearing up the Rookeries, by the look of it. The dog had leaped into action, and Sikes had followed it out of the back door and down the street, hat pulled down and scarf worn around as much of his face as he could hide.

The talking dog was Sikes' only friend, and he

guided him away from the trouble through the streets and the alleyways using all of his canine skills. The sounds of the police died down a bit, and Sikes called to Bullseye to stop so that they could make a plan. Bullseye heard his friend say something, and as he turned to ask him to repeat what he had said, the dog ran straight into a man, and they both went down in a heap. Sykes arrived, and once Bullseye had steadied himself they looked down at the man on the floor. He was well dressed and obviously not from these parts. He wasn't moving too well, and his breathing was shallow.

"Now look what you've gone and done, you stupid dog!"

"What I've done? This chap ran into me, William! And what's with this calling me a dog again? We were straight on this, weren't we? A dog I may be, but how many dogs do you know that can talk like what I do? So mind your manners, Bill, or you'll be working alone, my friend."

"Right you are, Bullseye, my apologies. Heat of the moment and all that. Those coppers back there have fairly put the wind up me. Has he got any valuables on him, then? Come on, we must be professional, mustn't we?"

Bullseye snuffled and pawed at the man on the ground. They picked him clean: his watch, watch chain, wallet and set of writing pens that looked very nice indeed were all swiftly removed from his person. They were just about to choose a canal to pitch him into when he started to mumble.

"Help me, please! My name is Charles Dickens. I must get to the Beaux Belles and meet up with Inspector Field… Dickens… Charles Dickens…"

Sikes looked at Bullseye in disbelief, then the dog looked up and into the face of the mumbling man that his despicable colleague was carrying over one shoulder. They looked at each other again, and Bullseye started to make one of his half-bark, half-laugh sounds.

Sikes slapped Bullseye's heavily-muscled rump.

"Well, well, well, what good luck for us, and what bad luck for Mr Charles Dickens! Quick now, Bullseye, we must go to ground sharpish."

13 ROYALTY AND SAUSAGES

It was the sound and the smell of the sausages that brought Judas back into the world of the living. He could hear the sizzling and the spattering of cooked pig's fat and he could smell at least 5 different sorts of animal flesh. His mouth watered, and his stomach gave a small leap to remind him that it needed filling. He tried to sit up, but the waves of nausea pushed him back onto the bed he was laying in. A cold flannel was placed on his forehead and he drifted away again, to dream of demons and a tree in a grove with a noose instead of olives on its branches.

When he finally woke again, the smell of the cooking had gone, and he had no idea what time it was. He had a vague recollection of being picked up and being moved. The pain had gone, and he was able to sit up without passing out. He was in a comfortable bed in a well-kept room. The sheets, pillows and blankets had that freshly-laundered smell, and the cotton crumpled in his ear as he moved his head around. The thick, heavy curtains at the window had been drawn aside so that some more of the feeble light could creep in. A quick look under the covers informed him that he was dressed, not in his own clothes but in some sort of robe that reached down past his knees and stopped just above the ankles.

He slipped out of the bed and drank all of the water in the jug on the stand in the corner of the room. The mirror above the stand showed him that he still had his looks – just. He was hungry, he was in one piece and he was very, very angry. If he had survived the falling wall then whatever the little demon chose to call itself was up and about, too.

Judas remade the bed; whoever had saved him and helped him to recuperate should be shown all the gratitude that he was able to muster. He opened the door to his room and found himself in a corridor with an equal amount of shiny wooden doors on either side. He reasoned he must be in some sort of guest house, or perhaps the nearest Police section house. Did he have Inspector Field to thank for coming back with reinforcements in the nick of time? He had no idea, and there were no visual clues as to his whereabouts, either. At the far end of the corridor was a curtain. It was purple in colour, and slid back and forth on brass rings attached to a brass bar. Judas walked up to it and pulled the curtains aside.

He did not have a member of the Metropolitan Police Force to thank for his rescue. Quite the opposite, it would seem. Behind the curtain was what appeared to be some sort of Royal Court. A throne sat upon a wooden dais at the far end of a huge loft. Little groups of men sat around tables, pointing at places on maps, while a string quartet played beautifully on the other side of the room. Runners raced back and forth with messages in hand. There was a huge wooden board leaning against a wall, covered in figures and times and details of everything from horse races to shipments of cargo from all over the world.

A young lady dressed in red and wearing a dark blue shawl around her shoulders saw him enter. She immediately made her excuses and disengaged from her little group, and walked over to him.

"I will let Lord Dodger know that you are up. When you see me beckon you may approach the throne, not before."

With that, she strode off. Judas followed at a discreet distance, and watched as the young lady waited her turn to speak. When called forward, she whispered her message into the ear of the man sitting on the throne. He listened intently, then looked up in Judas' direction. Their eyes met, and the man casually waved him over.

"So then, champion of the Rookeries, how do you fare? Are you mended?"

Judas couldn't work out if the man talking to him was a young man with the voice and bearing of someone much, much older, or if it was the other way around.

"My name is Judas Iscariot. May I ask who I am addressing so that I might give you my thanks for helping me?"

"My name is Lord Dodger. I used to have a first name, many years ago, but it has fallen away like old snow from the slates in February. You may call me Lord Dodger, the Little King, or even the Prince of the East. Lord, King or Prince. I don't mind, really."

"Lord Dodger, I am truly grateful for your assistance. There was another man with me when I fought the other... creature. Do you know if he survived, or where I might locate him?"

"I do know of his whereabouts and yes, he is alive, although he is not quite as healed as you, which has been playing on my mind somewhat these past three days. How is that a man can fight something that has killed so many, beat and subdue it, then recover fully even after a wall that was built with blocks of stone from Portland itself has fallen on him?"

Judas realised that the rest of the court had assembled behind him as they had been speaking. The silence was deafening.

"I have always been lucky, Lord Dodger."

"You are much more than that, my friend. They would have built you a pyre 50 feet high in these parts a hundred years ago.

"No matter. The beast has not been seen these past three days so we can assume that it has either slipped away into some deep and dark hole to die somewhere, is resting and planning its revenge on you, or something else entirely. If it resurfaces, I know who to send for. If it is dead, we can all rejoice. And if it comes looking for you, then I will know where it is going, and we shall run a book on you defeating it again. What do you say to that, Mr Iscariot?"

"My Lord, I am not going to wait for it to find me. If you allow me to go freely then I am in your debt. You can ask me to repay that debt, if it is lawful of course, and if there is another fight, depending on how quickly I can find the man who I was protecting the other night."

"Do you mean Mr Charles Dickens, the celebrated and soon to be famous novelist and teller of tales? A most talented scribe and, something tells me, the voice of an era and of a generation? If it is he you are looking for then he is being held by one William Sikes and his bodyguard, Bullseye. The latter is a talking dog the size of a Welsh pit pony and very nasty when riled. Whatever you do, don't call him a dog or treat him like one. The last person that stroked his head and offered to throw a stick for him to fetch lost two fingers.

"One of my men will give you the address where Mr Dickens can be found. You, Mr Iscariot, will owe me one small favour, repayable on request. If there is nothing more, I must return to the business of running my business. Fare well then, Mr Judas Iscariot. May good luck walk by your side, because you are far from the Temple on the Mount."

The last words were thrown away so casually that Judas heard them and processed them a fraction too late; before he could turn and ask what he had meant by them, the crowds of Lord Dodger's people had surged forward and ringed his throne, making any further dialogue impossible. As he walked away through the court, a note was pressed into his hand with two addresses written on it. He was also politely told that he could leave the nightshirt on the bed where he had slept, and that he would find his own clothes there – freshly laundered and pressed, of course.

After dressing and draining the water jug again, Judas was guided by the young lady in the red dress down a series of instantly forgettable corridors that led down and then up and left and then right, until he was completely lost. If the Metropolitan Police or a rival gang had cause ever to attack Lord Dodger's Kingdom, they would find themselves in the heart of a fiendish maze within minutes. It was a simple defensive strategy, but more reliable than a 50-foot high battlement. The young lady eventually stopped at one of the doors on the right. She tapped on it in some prearranged code, and the door opened into a storeroom piled high with boxes and barrels.

A couple of bruisers were playing crib on one of the upturned barrels in the centre of the room under a dirty skylight. Neither turned to look at him as he entered. He waited for his eyes to become accustomed to the light; as he did so, the door behind him closed with a soft click, and when he turned around the lady in the red dress was gone. He shook his head in the gloom, he had not heard her slip away and had wanted to at least thank her. But she was gone, and he needed to find Mr Charles Dickens, and make sure that he was safe.

When he turned back, the bruisers had stopped playing their card game. One of the pair had moved on silent feet to the other side of the storeroom, and now it was his turn to tap on his door with whatever today's code was. The door creaked open, and a shaft of light from the real world darted in like a thief. Judas walked across the room, acknowledging neither man as he felt it were somehow unprofessional to do so. He left the court of Lord Dodger behind, stepping out of his domain and into that of Queen Bustle and Strive. Her world was the busy crowd and the noisy street, and it was unrelenting and always restless. As Judas walked through the mass towards his lodgings, he wondered to himself why Lord Dodger had mentioned the Temple on the Mount.

14 THE RED QUILL

Charles Dickens woke up and realised immediately that he had escaped from one dangerous situation only to stumble blindly into another. His hands and feet were bound. His bonds were tight, but not painfully so. The room he was in was foreign to him, his wardrobe and writing desk were nowhere to be seen. In this dreary little place, a damp patch on the wall and a pile of rags on the floor occupied the spaces where his own, familiar furniture should be. It was dark, but not pitch black. The embers of a fire still glowed in the grate, and the air was thick with the heady bouquet of poverty and despair. His head hurt like hell, and throbbed as if to keep reminding him over and over again as to his folly. His left shoulder felt like it was on fire.

Whoever had made him fast to the bed, a very old,

wooden framed thing, was proficient with ropes and knots. An old sailor, perhaps? Dickens lifted his head from the mattress he was laying on, and tried to take in more of his current surroundings without attracting any interest from whoever had brought him here. He discovered that he was alone. He was excited and hopeful all in the same moment. He took a deep breath, and was just about to call for help, when the door was barged open and a huge growling shape that he had seen somewhere in his dreams, padded over to the bed, sticking its snout into his ear.

"One word, Mr Dickens, just one little word, and Bullseye – which is me, sir – will bite your ear off and wolf it down as you watch. Nice and quiet now, sir, my associate has a proposal for you.

"Here, Bill! Dickens has risen from his slumbers!"

"About bloody time and all," said a deep voice from the other room.

Dickens heard something heavy drop to the floor outside. Then, whatever floorboards that still remained on the floor and not in the fire started to squeak and complain, as the heavy form of Bill Sikes stumbled across them and into the room where Dickens was bound. William Sikes had been waiting for his treasure to wake up. He'd had enough of smelling what Bullseye had had for breakfast that morning; he wanted to get on with the business of ransoming Dickens and making enough money out of him to get away for a few weeks. The police were everywhere at the moment; double shifts were working the docks and the canal paths, while the Rookeries had been turned upside down and given a good shake. Things were bad, and the killer had struck twice more since they'd picked up their man. They had to move fast, or London would be as tight as a drum and no one would be getting out – at least not alive.

Sikes stomped into the room, roared, and threw his cudgel onto the pile of rags in the corner. It was all for effect, and normally it put the fear of the almighty into whoever he was threatening at the time. But it was all for naught, because a rat that was minding its own business underneath the rags was hit by accident and must have thought that the roof was caving in because it squeaked and shot out of its hiding place, straight into Bullseye's open jaws. Bullseye consumed it with two quick bites.

"For the love of all that is holy, Bullseye! Haven't you had enough to eat today?"

"No Bill, I haven't as it goes."

The huge dog looked defiantly at his friend, and yet Dickens could see that it was a little embarrassed at the same time. The tail of the rodent, at least the length of a decent bootlace and twice as thick, had been snipped off in the attack, and it had landed on Sykes' boot. Bullseye saw it at the same time as Sikes, and almost in an act of contrition the beast padded across the room to gingerly nibble it off.

"Your pardon, William…"

"Never mind that rat's tail, Bullseye, let's you and I get down to business. What shall it be, a finger or a toe?"

The dog's snout swung around very slowly, and his eyes locked with those of Mr Charles Dickens.

"I can whip a toe off as quick as a finger, Bill, makes no odds to me my friend. Just you give me the nod and it will be done as quick as two flashes."

The dog opened its mouth to reveal a set of nasty-looking yellow fangs. Some of the rat's flesh that it had just devoured was caught between them, and the stench that wafted across the bed to Dickens made him want to gag.

"I know you can, Bullseye, I has seen it with my own two eyes on many an occasion. But before you starts nibbling at Mr Dickens' digits, help me untie his hands. The writer must write his own ransom note, on account of the fact that I never learned my letters, and you my friend cannot hold a quill, which is a crying shame."

Two hours later at Scotland Yard, Inspector Field was handed a small parcel wrapped in dirty rags. It had been delivered anonymously and marked for his attention. Field unravelled the rags, which smelt disgusting, and then unwrapped the paper to reveal the little finger of a human male. Also in the package was a quill soaked in what could only be blood, and a note from Mr Charles Dickens, asking for the astronomical sum of £100 to be left in a carpet bag on the lip of the old well in Ivy Street at 12 o'clock the following day. All police were to be pulled out of the area, lest the body of the man who had written the note be chopped up and fed to a hungry beast.

"Well this has to be a first, Constable. It looks like whoever it was who snatched him made our friend Mr Dickens write his own ransom note, just before they had his finger off!

"This is the little finger from the left hand is it not? Tell me, Constable, do we know what hand Mr Dickens usually writes with? I sincerely hope that it's his right."

15 NOTES FOR A STORY

It took Judas longer than normal to wade through London's sea of people and traffic, but whatever it was that Lord Dodger and his followers had provided him with in the way of victuals, he was feeling surprisingly spry, and full of fettle. When he finally arrived at his lodgings, he found the maid from the previous day and a young Constable that had obvious designs on the girl waiting for him, with a letter from Inspector Field.

Judas took the message and retired to his room. He asked that the Constable wait for him while he dressed and picked up something that he needed. Once inside his room he checked to make sure that there were no nosy angels under the bed before opening the note.

He scanned the first few lines, then sat down at the

small table by the window to read it all again. Dickens had not made it to any of the cut-outs that they had discussed at the Belles. The Inspector had feared the worst, and ordered his men to make a sweep of the mortuaries. No bodies had been washed ashore on the mud flats of Wapping or the banks of the Thames, and nothing had been seen or heard of Dickens, until a ransom note had arrived at Scotland Yard. The details of the drop off point for the money were included on a separate sheet of paper.

Dickens was alive, missing the little finger of his left-hand, but still alive, nonetheless. He had not been killed by the demon, because demons have no interest whatsoever in financial gain. So good news so far, all things considered.

Judas continued to read the note and its supplementary instructions while making himself a cup of coffee. The maid had followed his instructions to the letter, thank goodness, and the messenger boy had collected some ground coffee beans he ordered from a Levantine merchant in Wapping.

He finished his second cup of the best coffee he had ever tasted this side of the Mediterranean Sea, sat back in his chair, and savoured the aromas of the region he had forfeited with his treachery. There was no immediate rush for him. The Inspector must watch the money, and save Mr Dickens. His own path was clear. He must find and destroy this demon, and if he could do the first in time to save Mr Dickens as well, then he would do whatever he could to help. It was obvious to him that the good men and women of this city, although valiant and brave, were ill-equipped to combat the evils of the underworld. Was this his fight? Did these people really need him? Were they *his* people? Judas sat still, breathed in deeply, and let the extra oxygen bring clarity to his troubled mind. He watched the ebb and flow of the innocents below on the street.

If you had asked him how he felt about people in general not so long ago, he would have been honest; he would have told you that they were all nothing to him, and that he really couldn't care less if they lived or died. But something had changed inside him. The rotten, black stone of selfishness that had grown inside him like some sort of malicious and malignant tumour had been reduced to a small, grey grain of indifference. Was he beginning to learn how to value the joy of life, and what it brings and teaches? He could have found an answer at the table by the window in his room, given time and peace and quiet. But the loud knocking on the door told him that right now, at this moment in time, with the forces of evil rampant and relentless and the lives of the innocent at risk, his fight was a physical one and not a metaphysical sit-by-the-window-and-think-positive-thoughts one.

He jumped up and changed into his new jacket, a coat that a team of tailors had made for him in a street that was called Saville Row, for some bizarre reason. Why had they called a street a 'Row'? The English language was very difficult to get to grips with. That was a question for another time, however, because the banging on his door had now become very, very persistent.

Judas turned back to the mirror that he had become close friends with. It was true, he was vain, and he enjoyed his own reflection, but the eyes that stared back out at him told him that there was a little boy out there with a demon inside him, and that demon needed cutting out and sending home. If they could save the boy after what it had seen and experienced, well, it would be a bonus.

Before he left he made sure that he was carrying the knife that the angel Littlewing had given him. Save the boy, save the writer if you can, and then try and save yourself.

16 THE FLOP HOUSE

Constable Benjamin was hot under the collar when he returned to the Yard. He'd run faster than he had ever done before in order to bring Inspector Field the note that this strange Mr Iscariot, the foreign looking gentleman, had jotted down for him. His urgency in getting across London so quickly was not just so that he could impress his commanding officer with his professional zeal. His steps were also full of adrenaline as he had fallen for the young maid that helped out at Mr Iscariot's lodging house. Kelly was her name and Constable Benjamin had told her, presumptuously, that he was at the vanguard of this dangerous investigation. Before leaving, he had made his pitch and said what he thought might win her heart.

"Dearest Kelly, if I should return unscathed from this desperate and dangerous endeavour, would you walk out with me this next Sunday coming on the Green at Bethnal? I may be wounded and hurt, but I would be honoured if you would take the hero of the hour on your arm."

She had looked at him, rolled her eyes, and nearly, almost, closed the door in his face. But just as he was about to admit defeat, she called out to him.

"The Green at Bethnal. I hope you like horses."

Inspector Field was not in the mood for lovesick heroes. Judas Iscariot had given the young constable a verbal message for the Inspector along with the note. An experienced man like Field would be able to combine the two communiques, and then use that intelligence to make the right decision. Unfortunately, Constable Benjamin had been concentrating on Kelly's dimples when he should have been concentrating on what Judas was planning, so he had forgotten the verbal part entirely.

"So, constable, this note that you took in hand from Mr Iscariot. It reads that someone called 'Lord Dodger' has given him the address of a flop house in a derelict part of 'The Rookeries'."

"That's right, sir."

"And then he goes on to say that he is going after the thing that attacked us the other night first. Right so far?"

"Yes, sir. That's right, sir."

"Then Mr Iscariot goes on to say something about a boy demon and a dull knife. His writing is a bit hurried, and what looks like the sweat from your palm has smudged the next bit so I can't read it properly. I presume he gave you a verbal message just in case the note was too go missing, constable?"

"Yes that's right, sir, demon boy knife dull flop house. That was it, word for word sir."

"There must have been some context or some other information? Does he require back up? Where exactly is the flop house, constable?"

The young policeman stared out of the window behind the Inspector's desk. He was affecting a quiet, nothing to add pose, and he wished at that moment with all his might that he was anywhere but Inspector Field's office. The Inspector could read all of his constables' faces like a children's book; he knew when to give them a rollicking, and when to save it for a more suitable time.

"Well then, constable, it looks like Mr Iscariot is going after a killer on his own. In the meantime, we shall put all of our energies into finding Mr Charles Dickens, before we have to stuff a carpet bag with pound notes and pay his ransom. You may go."

17 THE PEELER

The flop house that Lord Dodger's men had identified as the possible hiding place of the killer was every bit as derelict, dirty and downright rancid as Judas had expected. The building was barely standing, and torrents of rainwater cascaded down from the roof to splash noisily on the street below. The only door on the ground floor was being punished mercilessly by a number of draughts that ran through the building. It flapped and then cracked against the rotting timbers of the door frame. Directly in front of the opening, dogs had turned the white snow yellow. The few windows that remained were nailed shut.

Judas was not going to enter the building through the front door. He could see that the stairs were a death trap, too, and he had no intention of getting caught up in a fight with this thing on ground that he wouldn't trust to hold a feather up. The building next to the flop house looked slightly sturdier, and there were hauling posts protruding from the warehouse doors at the top with ropes hanging from them. He could always swing across up there, and gain entrance to the flop house through one of the holes that used to be windows. If the creature was there he would deal with it; if he were in any fit state after that, he would find Dickens, and finally pay a call on the old businessman.

The stairs in the building next to the flop house had seen better days, but they were solid, and he made it to the top of the building swiftly. As he had expected, there was no door between the two buildings; it looked like the only way in would be on the end of a rope. Judas grabbed one and pulled down on it as hard as he could. He half expected it to snap and fall away, but it held firm. He grasped the rope with both hands, took aim at the empty window of the flop house opposite, and launched himself out of the warehouse.

The second that his feet left the floor, his scar began to burn like crazy. As he swung towards the window of the flop house, he immediately spotted the boy.

In another time the boy may have reached out to help him, but unfortunately, this wasn't that time and the demon inside the boy was out for his blood. As Judas swung towards him the demon smiled through the boy's mouth. It stepped forward, and threw itself out of the window, catching Judas in mid-air. Judas was trying to hang on, and the demon was trying to twist his head off.

Judas had had enough already, and he calmly released his grip on the rope. The white ground with the yellow dots on it came up to meet them both. The impact was terrible, smashing all the remaining breath from his lungs. The demon was on its feet first, and for the first time since he had met it, Judas was overjoyed. The demon had been causing havoc and putting the fear of God into all and sundry without consequence, and it was over-confident. Judas waited for it to clamber onto him, then reached into his coat pocket for the knife he had been given. It wasn't there.

The demon had him by the throat now, the small hands of the boy delivering a grip of iron. Judas was starting to wonder if the demon had the power to kill him properly, when he suddenly realised that he had put the knife in his coat pocket when it was hanging up on the coat stand, not when he was already wearing it. So, he reached into his other pocket in case he'd slipped it in there by mistake. There it was. He would have laughed at his own stupidity, but the sky was getting darker and his limbs were going limp.

When the demon saw the knife, looking like no more than a potato peeler or something for getting stones of horses hooves, it began to cackle manically.

"That pin sticker will not trouble me! I'll twist your head off before it cuts me!"

Judas looked at it again. He had to hand it to the demon, it did look small and flimsy, and he doubted whether it would be able to cut through a banana in its current form, let alone a creature from the underworld. But just as Littlewing had promised, the knife knew that it was needed. The next moment, Judas was holding a flaming sword, and the moment after that, it was piercing straight through the boy's chest. The demon roared, its grip weakened around Judas' throat, then it fell away and collapsed on the floor at his feet. Judas looked at the flaming sword and couldn't resist giving it a swish in the air to see what sound it made. He got one or two nice passes in, before the demon vanquisher returned to its former diminutive state.

Judas put the knife back in his pocket, and looked down at the boy. He could not sense the demon at all, and his scar was silent. Nevertheless, he picked the body in front of him up, and removed it to the nearest Church he could find, where he ordered the priest to watch over it until he returned.

18 MAN'S BEST FRIEND

The day was ending, and the pure white snow had started to fall once again. It softened the city, making it appear more magical. If you were in a wistful frame of mind, you might even say it looked beautiful.

Inspector Field watched the snowflakes through the window of the Pawn Shop they had chosen as their place to survey the hand-over of the ransom money. Almost all of his serving officers were on duty now, stationed at key points in order to catch whoever it was that was sent to collect the money. This huge sum had been donated by the good people of the city, with some of it even coming from the Met itself. The Christmas party at the Yard would be a bit thin this year because of it.

The terms of the collection had been set by the

kidnappers. A heavy-duty carpet bag was to be filled with the money, and it was to be left on the edge of the well at the bottom of Ivy Street, in plain view. There it sat now, not more than 50 yards away from the Inspector's vantage point. He'd seen the great stacks of pound notes at the Bank of England, but had never carried that much money himself. He had checked the full bag three times, surprised at how heavy it was.

When the bag had been collected at the allotted time and the money was all accounted for, the kidnappers would release Mr Dickens with all of his remaining digits intact. If there was any attempt to interfere by the Police, however, Mr Dickens would never lift a pen again.

Inspector Field shook his head in disbelief at the lengths that some people would go to for money. He was just about to take a quick nip from his hip flask to keep the cold at bay, when one of his Constables edged into the room and theatrically tip-toed across to him.

"There's a man downstairs says that you know him, and he has some news for you, sir. Says his name is Chariot, sir. James Chariot I think, sir."

Inspector Field ordered one of his men to keep an eye on the bag and alert him if anything happened, then went down to see Mr Chariot.

"I can tell you that the killer is no more, Inspector," said Judas.

"All we need to do now is to capture whoever the kidnappers are and save Mr Dickens. Has there been any movement or attempt to take the money,

Inspector? The streets I passed through to get here are almost empty; it would take a brave man or a very stupid one to think that he could just wander up and take the bag."

"Nothing so far, Mr Iscariot. I am a might perturbed though as to the position of the money. It's right out there in the open, and as you say, impossible to take without anyone noticing."

In the sewers under Ivy Street, Bill Sikes and Bullseye, his friend and canine accomplice, were waiting for the sound of the bells to ring out from the nearby Church. It was the signal they were waiting for, the one that would tell them that the night was on its way. They were sitting on top of a dry-stone wall with a flask of gin and a packet of open sandwiches between them. The only thing missing was the sky and some countryside to go with their picnic. Bullseye couldn't help himself, and he let out a windy fart that had Sikes reaching for his handkerchief in order to cover his mouth and nose again.

"I thought this here sewer stank but you Bullseye, you are a rotter!"

"It's the ham Bill, the ham. You know it always makes me windy and unpleasant to be around. It's your fault for making the sandwiches with it!"

"You are an ungrateful dog, Bullseye, and mark my words you will be on your own if you don't start to respect your betters."

Bullseye's hackles went up instantly. He'd heard

that insult once too many times from Sikes and he was angry now. A low growl sounded at the back of his throat. Sikes was not about to back down, either, and let his hand drop to his coat pocket, where he always kept his trusty repeater. But just then the church bells sounded, and that meant that it was time to get rich. They could tear each other apart later, and to the victor the spoils.

They crept along the sewer until they found the entrance to the tunnel that they had been looking for, and climbed inside. At the end of this tunnel there was hatch made of moonlight, and they crawled towards it. Sikes removed his hat; he very carefully edged his head through it and looked up at the circle of the night sky, shining down from the top of the Ivy Street well that now stood directly above them. Snowflakes floated down towards them, and Sikes watched one as it passed him by and settled briefly on the surface of the water at the bottom of the well before disappearing. The tunnel here entered the well about six feet above the water and ten feet from the top, and they could see the lovely fat black shape of the bag sitting there in the moonlight, waiting to be plucked.

The plan was that Sikes would climb up the rope that was attached to the bucket, then switch the bag with the money in it for a bag that looked just like it but was full of old newspaper. The police would continue to watch the wrong bag, and they would be long gone before they were rumbled. It was genius. He climbed up the rope, and Bullseye handed him the substitute bag. Bill was very strong, and had no trouble at all in swapping the bags very quickly, whilst still hanging on to the rope and remaining unseen. He switched the bags, and threw the money down to Bullseye. The Mastiff looked inside and gave out a little, excited yap. Bill heard it, and then started climbing back down the rope towards the mouth of the tunnel, and their escape. He descended, hand over hand, but just before he could swing himself into the tunnel Bullseye leaned out, and bit him on the thigh. His bite was so strong that he drew blood straight away, and Sikes tumbled into the water at the bottom of the well.

"You won't be calling me a 'foul dog' no more now, will you William, my friend!"

The head and shoulders of one William Sikes, bad man and underground enforcer emerged from the water. The first look on his face was that of surprise. The next was sheer fury, and he launched himself up at his accomplice. But he was treading water, and there was no firm ground to push away from so he simply floundered. He snarled, and tried to climb up the smooth wet wall of the well, but it was no use. There weren't any handholds to grip, or steps to place a boot on, and by now the many pockets of his coat were filling with water. He realised that he was going to drown.

"You backstabber! You filthy flea-bitten, stinking dog! You cur! I'll find you, Bullseye, just you wait!"

Sikes curses were delivered in vain, because

Bullseye was already gone, and the money was gone with him.

He continued to bellow and cry out for help until he found himself being rescued by the constables that Inspector Field had stationed at the end of the street. Sikes was well-known so they took their time, and he was waterlogged and as weak as a kitten by the time they pulled his heavy frame over the lip of the well. Inspector Field was livid that the money had gone, but he had caught one of the kidnappers, and when you have one criminal in custody it is only a matter of time before you have their accomplices.

Judas watched Field and his constables in action, and he liked what he saw. They were a good group of men and London was fortunate to have them. He joined them as they made their way back to Scotland Yard. As they rode in the back of a police Maria, Judas had an urge to ask Field what the link was between the yard at the back of the station and Scotland, but the look on Field's face suggested that maybe another time would be best for asking odd questions.

When they arrived at the station, Sikes was taken down to the cells straight away and given some warm clothing to change into, along with a mug of hot punch. He took both gladly, but refused to answer any of Field's questions regarding Dickens, which started to sound alarm bells in the Inspector's mind.

Field stepped away from the bars of the cell that they were holding Sikes in and motioned for Judas to follow him out of the cell block. As soon as they entered Field's office, the Inspector flopped down into one of the chairs by the fire, removing his boots and lifting the soles of both feet up to the flames.

"We spent a lot of money on these uniforms, you know: leather belts, good broadcloth tunics that keep the chills out, and capes for when it gets really bitter. But these boots are going to cripple us if we don't do something about them!"

Judas smiled. He sat down in the chair opposite the Inspector, held both of his hands out, and flexed his fingers.

"The man Sikes is not likely to talk, is he? He looks a hard man."

"One of the worst I'm afraid, Mr Iscariot. His accomplice is almost certainly a giant bull mastiff called Bullseye. They're practically inseparable, and it appears to me at first glance that something has gone awry between them, hence the muttering and the pacing going on down in that cell."

"Do we know where to find the dog, Inspector? Do that, and we'll possibly find the money, and then Dickens?"

"Bullseye will be long gone by now, Mr Iscariot. That hound has friends in low places, and I fear that trying to find him could take up valuable time, and ultimately mean the death of our friend Mr Dickens. We need to get Sikes to talk."

Judas sat back in his chair and looked into the flames of the fire for an answer to their current predicament. The flames danced and twisted, and

Judas watched as piece of kindling fell out of the fire onto the tiled hearth. The small, thin piece of wood burned brightly for a second, then it died. When it was extinguished, Judas knew how to get Sikes to talk.

"Inspector, I may have an idea that will get Sikes to talk. But I'm going to have to ask you to trust me to speak to Sikes on his own."

The Inspector tried to make himself more comfortable in his chair by removing a rather lovely embroidered cushion from behind his back. He saw Judas looking at it and appeared a little embarrassed.

"A present from my good lady wife, Mr Iscariot. I try not to let the rank and file see my little home comforts if possible because it would be round the station faster than a bout of the common cold, and they would no doubt all find it incredibly amusing.

"I have no problem with you interviewing Sikes on your own, as long as he remains on one side of the bars and you on the other. If you have something else in mind then that might prove more difficult. Sikes is a dangerous, evil man, and he will kill you if he has the chance, even in here."

"Thank you for your concern, Inspector, but I have certain safeguards in place, and it will prove very difficult, nigh impossible, for Mr Sikes to kill me. I think that I could show him something that will make him talk. But I cannot share it with you or any of your men. You have my word that Sikes will remain unharmed. He may babble about some strange things afterwards, but you can disregard them as the ramblings of a crazy man recently fished out of a deep well."

The Inspector turned in his chair and looked at Judas intently. He was weighing up the consequences of losing the ransom money, Dickens, and possibly even Mr Iscariot, too. The money he couldn't care less about, but Dickens could be laying in some cellar somewhere having his toes removed one by one as punishment for spoiling the plan. Field would never have risked another soul, but there was something about this man that the Inspector liked. So he decided to trust him.

"Along with a few of my most capable men, I will be waiting on the other side of the door, Mr Iscariot. At the first sign of any danger we will enter and subdue Sikes. Is that clear?"

Judas nodded, and stood up to leave.

"Hang on, there. I need to get my boots back on," said the Inspector.

19 BILL THE PEACH

Bill Sikes was livid. Faithful Bullseye, his friend, had double-crossed him and made off with £100! Half of that belonged to Bill, and he wanted it back.

Bullseye would cover Gypsy Joe Rose's cut for sending the job their way, and the blasted hound would still have £80! Damn him. He'd chop the dog into rat meat when he caught up with him. They could send him over to the Fleet or Newgate Prison now if they wanted to, but he could get out of both as easy as kiss his own hand. And then he'd come for Bullseye's throat.

Sikes had started to think of new and very slow ways to kill Bullseye, but his inner dialogue was suddenly brought to a halt when he heard the ominous clang of the bolt being drawn on the steel door that opened on to the cell block. He looked up, expecting to see Field and some of his lads with their truncheons drawn. Instead, only one man was standing there, and he didn't look like any policeman that Sikes had seen before.

The man stepped forward into the light so that he could see Sikes, and Sikes could see him. Bill heard the steel door closing, followed by the muffled scraping of the bolt being pushed back into place. The cell block was secure once more.

"Where's Field?"

Bill was in no mood for pleasantries or games.

"Inspector Field has allowed me to come and ask you a few questions. And to enlighten you if you decide not to help us with our enquiries."

"Oh he has, has he? You can tell Field that he'll get nothing from me. He'd be better off sending me over to the Fleet."

Bill stood up and moved closer to the bars. If the other man stepped any closer then Bill would be able to reach through them, grab the odd-looking cove by the lapels, and pull him into the iron rails. When Bill had smashed his brains in, maybe Field would stop messing about.

Judas had been dealing with men like Sikes for many years now. He'd fought them in different countries, with different weapons, and in far too many prisons and cells just like this one. Sikes was seriously out of his class, and he didn't even know it. Judas sighed, and started to ask the questions, even though he knew that Sikes would not answer them yet.

"Where is Charles Dickens?"

Silence.

"Where is Mr Charles Dickens, Bill?"

Silence.

"If you tell me where he can be found, Mr Sikes, it will go better for you."

Silence.

"I'll tell you what, Bill. I'll fight you for the information. Hand-to-hand, in there. Just you and me. How does that sound?"

The grin that appeared on William Sikes' face would have made a wolf happy. He looked at the man on the other side of the bars, and he liked what he saw. He'd fought with knives, metal prison buckets, staves, and stones, and here he was, still standing, while all the others he'd fought had perished.

"I'll take you up on that, my friend. If you have a spare pair of knives about you, we could really make this worth my while."

Judas reached into the pocket of his long coat and pulled out two knives. One was a short, stubby-looking thing, while the other was a standard issue police bayonet with a truly fine, razor-sharp edge. Bill looked at both and smiled.

"Well, that's as expected isn't it now. You get the big, nasty pig-sticker and Bill here gets the breadknife that has seen better days. That's right, isn't?"

It was Judas' turn to smile. He casually tossed the bayonet into the cell.

"Not quite, Mr Sikes. I think I will take a chance on this stub of steel. If I can bring you down and you yield to me, then you tell me where I can find Dickens. If by some feat of magic and skill you best me, then you get to walk out of here. Sound agreeable?"

Bill was fairly hopping up and down with excitement. This man must have just escaped from Bedlam! To think he could beat William Sikes in a knife fight!

"Come on in then, your honour. And apologies in advance for ruining your suit and cutting your heart out."

Judas weighed the knife in his hand, opened the cell door, and stepped inside.

Inspector Field was waiting anxiously behind the steel door behind them. He'd heard the two men mumbling from inside, and assumed that Sikes had gone professionally deaf like the criminal he was. Then he heard the cell door opening, and cursed himself for a fool. His men yanked on the bolt that made the door fast, and wrenched it open.

As they all piled in there was a sudden flare of light so bright that they all threw themselves down on the floor and covered their heads. The light was so bright that each of them needed to place cold, wet flannels on their faces for hours afterwards. Inspector Field swore blind that he saw Mr Judas Iscariot with a long sword that was made of fire before he was forced to dive for cover. A few of the other men later swore they'd seen lightning in the hands of Mr Iscariot, held aloft over the head of Sikes. Whatever it was, William Sikes, legendary hard man and famous knife fighter, was reduced to a babbling wreck on the floor of his cell.

Before Bill was taken up the stairs and away to Newgate, he told Judas and Inspector Field where to find Dickens, as well as peaching on all of his known associates. A Black Maria was despatched to collect Dickens, and within the hour, he was being ushered into Inspector Field's office and told to sit by the fire to recover himself. The worst had passed, and he was safe again.

After seeing his hand treated by the police surgeon, Dickens became quite animated. The third glass of brandy on an empty stomach might have been the cause, but nevertheless he spoke at length about his adventures over the past couple of days, and all of the things that he had seen. He said he had enough material and stimulation to write any number of books.

Judas shook the hand that still contained all its fingers, and was about to take his leave, when Charles Dickens took him to one side, and asked him a very important question.

"Mr Iscariot, may I write a story with you in it? There is so much to tell of our adventures: Sikes and Bullseye, Lord Dodger the King of the pickpockets, malevolent spirits, subterfuge, deceit and kidnap! It would make an amazing tale, and you would be at the heart of it all."

Judas smiled kindly at the writer, savouring the goodwill that Dickens wanted to lavish upon him. It had been quite a while since anyone had thought this well of him, but his fight must go on, and he must be able to move freely in the underworlds. If his name and his purpose was known too soon then he would fail. So he politely declined, and asked Inspector Field to encourage Dickens not to make his name popular, as his livelihood depended upon it. They agreed to allow certain details to be immortalised in print and for others to be forgotten. Judas shared a drink with the two men, then left and made his way back to his lodgings for a good night's sleep. He had an appointment with an old businessman tomorrow, and a priest who was keeping an eye on a demon for him.

20 CHRISTMAS PRESENT

The tap on the door to his room the following morning was so soft a mouse could have done better. Judas was already wide awake, though, so didn't miss it, and he opened the door for the maid so that she could deliver a pot of his coffee to the table. He was careful enough to keep his scarred stomach from view, and she kept both eyes on the floor for most of the time she was in his room.

After he had drunk his coffee and dressed, he sat by the window once again and stared out of the window. The world was still turning, and hopefully there was one less demon in it. Add to that the safe return of Dickens and the incarceration of Sikes, the makings of a good day were all in place.

His appointment with the old businessman was set for six o'clock that evening. He'd asked for the kitchen boy at his lodgings to take a note around first thing and the reply had come back with him. Icing sugar dusted his lips on his return, and when questioned he'd told the head of the lodging staff that the old man had made him take a sugar sweet in the shape of mouse with icing sugar for whiskers for his troubles. That sounded just like the man, thought Judas, as he made his way around the perimeter of the Rookeries. He had no desire to wander those streets on his own for a while, so he kept to the streets and the lanes that encircled them and found his way to the small Catholic church where he'd left the boy's body without taking too many wrong turns.

The young priest whose church it was greeted him at the door with a welcoming smile. Judas liked him straight away. He could see that they both had a lot in common, apart from the smile. The priest led Judas down the aisle and when he reached the altar, the clergyman took a knee and made the sign of the cross. Judas followed suit. He'd done enough damage already. He followed the priest to the back of the church and into a small set of rooms where he and his wife lived, and where they tended to their flock.

The young boy was sitting at their kitchen table, spooning copious amounts of broth into his mouth. He didn't look up as they entered. The priest nodded at the boy, then gestured for Judas to follow him back into the church. They both sat down on a pew near the front door.

"So, Father, how does the boy do?"

The Priest reached for the crucifix around his neck and Judas feared the worst, but it was just one of the comforting actions that people perform when they want to think or order their thoughts.

"He slept for the remainder of the night after you left him here, and then for most of yesterday. He's eating well and the scared, look on his face has gone.

"Something awful happened to that boy, and he seems, God willing, to be healing in his own fashion. He knows his own name, but apart from that, his past is hazy to him. He thinks he had a mother once, and that is where I shall start my search for his parents.

"I performed the act of exorcism on the boy, as you instructed. Something was there. I felt it for a second, but I am sure that it is gone now."

Judas shifted on his pew, looked up at the altar, and nodded.

"Thank you, Father, you've saved the boy and many lives that could have been in danger if the spirit inside him had not been cast out. May I speak with him?"

The priest got up, walked backdown the aisle, took the knee again, and then disappeared into the rooms at the back of the church. Moments later, he returned with the boy. He was going to break some hearts when he was older, that was for sure. Blonde hair, blue eyes and a flawless complexion. Very different to the face that Judas had seen before. The boy seemed to recognise Judas, too, but he decided not to remind him of the circumstances of their previous encounter.

"The good Father here is going to look after you for a while. I can think of no better place for you to be than under God's roof. In time you may remember me, or perhaps not. All the same, it is fair that you should know my name, which is Judas Iscariot."

God had made sure that Judas carried his guilt and his shame with him wherever he went in the world. He had made it so that Judas could shout his name as loudly as he could in the biggest Church in all the land, but everyone would hear 'John Brown' or 'Joe Black', instead. He was clever that way.

The boy nodded, then walked away in search of more broth. Before he left, Judas made a donation to the church.

"Father, here is a purse of money for the boy. I'm sure he'll have many more adventures, but he deserves a good start. This other purse is for you and the church. You have done me and the boy a great service."

Judas was halfway down the path when something occurred to him. He turned around.

"What name will the boy go by, Father?"

The Priest smiled.

"He knows that his first name is Oliver, and that he thinks his second might have something to do with twisting. Twist, or twisted? So he has decided on Oliver Twisted."

Judas wanted to suggest something else, but if the boy had no recollection of the demon and the way in which it liked to twist people's heads off, then maybe he shouldn't draw attention to it. The priest weighed the first bag of money in his hand and then the other.

"This will make the next few days more bearable for my congregation and the people hereabouts, the poor souls find it particularly hard at this time of year. Tonight is Christmas Eve, after all, and I would like to give them all a good, hot meal and a few pennies. I find the promise of some reward for their time makes them more attentive to my sermon for some reason. Go with God, and a Merry Christmas to you Sir."

He left the priest to his flock, and walked away through the graveyard. He was saddened to see that most of the graves in the graveyard were for children who had not lived past the age of 12. One day, life might last longer, perhaps.

Judas had allowed enough time so that he would be precisely on schedule for his last appointment. And as he walked through the city, he was amazed at how much the people made, with so little. They were cold, hungry most of the time, and worked hard just to stay alive, but at this time of the year something changed within them. The whole city was alive with festivities and joy, and music and laughter. Maybe people weren't so bad after all?

The butler held the door open as he approached, and he was no sooner through the main door and into the hallway when his coat and hat were taken, and a steaming tankard of mulled wine was pressed into his hand to help chase the cold night air away. The house was full of people. But it was no ordinary Christmas party, it seemed. There were people here in fine evening dresses and tailored suits with black tie rubbing shoulders with the ordinary folk, those people that lived different lives but deserved to be recognised all the same. Judas circulated and made what little small talk he possessed. When the dinner gong was sounded and the maids and the serving staff were encouraging everyone to make their way to the banquet table, he felt a tug at his elbow.

"Good evening, Judas. How lovely to see you again."

Littlewing was dressed in an immaculate suit. His shoes alone must have cost as much as the national debt, and his wings weren't visible.

"That's a neat trick, Littlewing. Where are those wings of yours? Not lost them, have you?"

"Oh, you can be incredibly vexing. The Archangel warned me about that. The wings are there, but people who are not entirely in the club, as it were, are unable to see them properly."

Littlewing escorted Judas into the main hall, and as if by magic, Judas discovered that he would be sitting right next to the angel at dinner. What a coincidence, he thought to himself.

The dinner started well, and became legendary thereafter. All the social classes mixed, and they forgot about their stations in life, throwing themselves into making new friendships instead. During the meal, Littlewing made small talk about the City of the Heavens, and of angels and people that he and Judas might have in common. It was not until just before the dessert was served that he delivered his message.

"He has decided that you are to stay here in this city, Judas. No more searching and wandering for the moment. He wants you stay here.

"The old businessman will ask you to join him for brandy and cigars shortly. He has had an idea, and he has been looking for someone like you to help him with it. He's going to introduce you to a like-minded spirit that just happens to be on a similar path to you. Have a lovely evening, and goodnight, Judas."

Littlewing excused himself, and sauntered away into the crowd with a glass of champagne in one hand and a young lady's hand in the other.

The butler approached, and using the most immaculate etiquette, waited for a lull in the conversation around them before leaning over Judas' shoulder.

"My master, Mr Ebenezer Scrooge, begs five minutes of your time, sir."

Also by Martin Davey:

Judas the Hero

The Children of the Lightning

The Curious Case of Cat Tabby

Printed in Great Britain
by Amazon